Copyright © 2018

ISBN-13: 978-1722405182

ISBN-10: 172240518X

Matt Shaw Publications

All rights reserved. This book or any portion thereof may not be reproduced or used in any manner whatsoever without the express written permission of the publisher except for the use of brief quotations in a book review.

The characters in this book are purely fictitious.

Any likeness to persons living or dead is purely coincidental.

www.mattshawpublications.co.uk
www.facebook.com/mattshawpublications

The First Cuddle

Exclusive to KillerCon 2018

Matt Shaw

This book is exclusive to KillerCon 2018.
It is limited to 250 copies.
This is copy number ___18___ of 250

A huge thank you to Wrath James White for inviting me to be a part of this convention. You, sir, are a gent. (Although I could totally kick your butt if I wanted to… I just choose not to. Cough)

Signed

Matt Shaw

The baby had been born prematurely after what had been a traumatic pregnancy. At week thirty-five the baby was in breech position; its feet pointed downwards and its head up. When an ECV failed to correct the baby's position, the doctors had told her she'd need a caesarian as it would be safer than a natural birth. It wasn't a prospect which filled Chloé with joy but - they knew best. It was her first child and she was already scared to death, not helped by the fact her real mother had died during childbirth. At week thirty-seven Chloé went into premature labour and by the time she got to the hospital, it was too late to have the baby any other way but through natural means.

Chloé closed her eyes as she tried to put everything from mind. As she did so, another tear welled from her eye. It snaked its way down her cheek and dripped off onto her hospital gown.

It's over now, she thought to herself.

A nurse asked, 'Are you ready to hold your baby now?'

Chloé kept her eyes closed a moment longer before slowly opening them. She looked towards the nurse who was standing by the bed. In her arms there was a little wrapped bundle. Chloé could see the top of the baby's pink head. Nervously, she nodded to the nurse.

The nurse leaned down and carefully handed the baby over to Chloé who was no longer able to hold back the tears as she took her child for the first time.

'Hey baby,' Chloé said.

The nurse asked, 'Have you thought of a name yet?'

Chloé didn't answer her. She just held the baby closer to her, not wanting to ever let him go now that he was finally there with her. The nurse took the lack of response as the new mum wanting to be left alone.

'I'll be close by,' she said.

Chloé nodded. Another tear dribbled from her eye as the nurse turned and left the immediate area. Chloé looked down to the little pink head poking from the top of the clinical looking blanket.

'Hello,' she said, 'I'm your mummy…'

She leaned down and kissed the babe on the top of his cold head. Struggling to stop herself screaming, she turned to her partner who'd been standing close-by the whole time. He too had tears in his eyes which looked as though they were too sore to be open. No doubt he had been crying the whole time she'd been under for her operation. He tried his best to force a reassuring smile.

'Did you want to hold him?' Chloé asked.

He shook his head despite knowing - in time to come - it would be a move he would come to regret. As it stood though, he just couldn't bring himself to do it.

'Excuse me a minute,' he said with a slight crack in his voice.

Chloé watched as he left the room, leaving her and their son alone for the first time. She looked back at her baby.

Tinged with sadness, she gave him another kiss on the top of his head and said, 'I'm sorry.'

Carefully she laid him down upon her lap. Such was the medication flowing through her veins that she could barely feel his weight there. Even if there wasn't a numbness to her body, she wasn't sure if she'd have felt his weight there though: He was so small.

Even more carefully, she slowly peeled away the hospital blanket as though she was undoing the wrapping to a fragile and expensive gift. His skin was so pale looking, not helped by the blue glow of the overhead luminescence. She noticed the little scarf around his neck, which she told herself was to keep him warm. She looked at the nappy they'd put on him, a couple of sizes too big due to his size. She looked at his little hand; fingers folded in gripping thin air. So tiny. So still. Chloé slid her index finger into the little boy's non-existent grip and - with her other hand - gently tried to close his fingers around her own, if only to try and imagine him holding her just one time. The fingers didn't stay in position for long, slowly curling back to their original position.

Chloé pulled her own finger away before she got too upset by the baby's lack of grip. As she put her hands either side of the baby's body, she couldn't help but notice the tiny little foot. It looked so small here and now and yet it had felt huge as she'd earlier pushed it out of herself; her vagina stretched, and ripping to the point of needing stitches, in the unpleasant - and painful - process of child-birth. How could something so small do so much damage? One foot first and then - helped by the doctor - the second. Chloé tried to push the memory from her mind as it caused her body to ache despite the pain meds she was on. This tiny little foot.

The nursing team had already offered to make a foot and hand print for Chloé to take home with her. A poor substitute given the fact she'd been expecting to carry the child home. Even so, it was better than going home empty-handed with only stitches and pain as a memory to the child that should have been.

She stroked the little boy's foot, tickling the sole. Would he have been ticklish? Would there have been occasions when she would've had him screaming with laughter as she playfully pinned him? She smiled at the thought of what could have been despite the image being a double-edged sword. On one hand it was nice to think about and on the other - she knew it would never be. Chloé put both hands around the little child's feet and gave them a gentle and loving squeeze. As she did so, the midwife's voice popped into her head.

'You can't just pull them.'

Chloé tried to close her mind to the memory but it was there now, lodged and stuck with her for life along with the feeling of pressure as the delivering doctor pulled upon the baby's legs in an effort to try and pull him from within her. Even with the meds she could still feel that pressure as though reliving it. The stretching of the skin around the vagina, the widening of the birth canal, the internal scraping as the infant was pushed as best she could towards the opening and what should have been its new life.

Chloé let out a little cry of pain; emotions brought about from physical pain and emotional turmoil. She looked back down to the little lifeless baby and openly wept. As the emotions continued flooding from her, her mind kept replaying what had happened: The feeling of the doctor pulling upon the newborn, the cautionary words of the mid-wife advising against it and then - worse - the feeling of the pressure just suddenly stopping as the baby's body was pulled from inside her.

Chloé - distraught and hoping everything had been nothing but a dream - started to unravel the small scarf around the child's neck. Her heart skipped a beat when she saw the small stitches piercing the pale skin at the mid-mark of the neck and, again, her cruel mind kicked into overdrive with the replaying of the mid-wife's scream and the feeling... *That* feeling that, although the pressure was gone and the doctor was holding her baby's limp body, her insides still felt as though they were full.

She'd screamed too when she saw the blood spurting from the baby's neck stump. Thick jets of dark red claret over both the doctor's uniform and shocked expression. It was a scream which changed pitch when she realised what was still inside her. A scream which turned from a high shriek to pleading words begging for them to get it out of her as she started to imagine what she believed to be the sound of a newborn's crying coming from between her legs.

'Get it out of me! Get it out of me!' Chloé's yelling brought the nurses running back into the room and the door slamming behind them snapped the traumatised patient back to the present and the supposedly-reassuring words of the nurses telling her that it was going to be okay.

One of the nurses tried to take the baby away from her.

'Don't you fucking touch him!' Chloé yelled. The pain, the fear, the shock - all starting to manifest itself into anger and hatred. What had happened had been a tragic accident, it wasn't their fault. Not the midwife or nurses. She didn't blame them. The blame she rested solely on the doctor. He was the one who'd pulled the baby with too much force, yanking the body clean away from the head. Not them. Him. Regardless, Chloé had no intention of letting them take her boy now that she had him.

She bundled him back up in his little blanket and pulled herself, painfully, from the bed. As she did so, she pulled the stitches from the emergency C-Section she'd had to remove her son's head from within. Chloé - running on adrenaline and fear - didn't even cry out.

One of the nurses said, 'It's okay, take it easy…' but her words fell upon deaf ears. 'Where are you going?' The nurse was obviously concerned and only had the best of intentions, wanting to help Chloé but - to Chloé - she only wanted to take her baby away.

'You can't have him,' Chloé said. 'You can't take him away. He's mine! I won't let you take him…'

'It's okay… It's okay… No one wants to take your baby…'

Chloé looked towards the doors of the private room. There was no clear path there, because the nurses were blocking the way. Even if she could make it there though - she knew it wasn't an exit which would allow her to remain with her son. The only exit which would permit that was on the other side of the room.

'Just get back into bed…'

Chloé turned to the closed window and - without a second thought - threw herself at it. The nurses screamed out as the glass shattered around her. Sharp shards cut deep gouges in the flesh over various parts of

Chloe and the baby's body as her weight took them both through and plummeting to the floor two stories down. One shard had nicked one of the stitches holding the boy's now flapping head to his body and by the time mother and son smashed into the concrete below - none of the stitches were able to do their job. Her insides were spread out for all to see and the baby's head rolled a few feet away from his contorted body. As the head came to a stop, his eyes were fixed on his mother. His mother's still eyes fixed on him.

Thank you to those of you who came along to see me at the convention. Your support means the world to me and makes all the travel worthwhile!

If you enjoyed this story and would like to read more – you can find my work readily available on Amazon.

Well, most of it… They banned some of it…

Safe travels home and, thank you again.

www.mattshawpublications.co.uk

www.facebook.com/mattshawpublications

Made in the USA
San Bernardino, CA
06 August 2018